In the Ghost Detective Universe:

Novels
(Best to be read in order)
Beyond the Grave
Unveiling the Past
Beneath the Surface
Piercing the Veil

Short Stories
(All stand-alone)
Just Desserts
Lost Friends
Family Bonds
Common Ground
Till Death
Family History
Heritage
New Beginnings
Far From Home
Severed Ties
Eternal Bond
Harsh Expectations
Dull Expectations

Short Story Collections
Unfinished Business, Vol 1

R.W. WALLACE

Author of *Beyond the Grave*

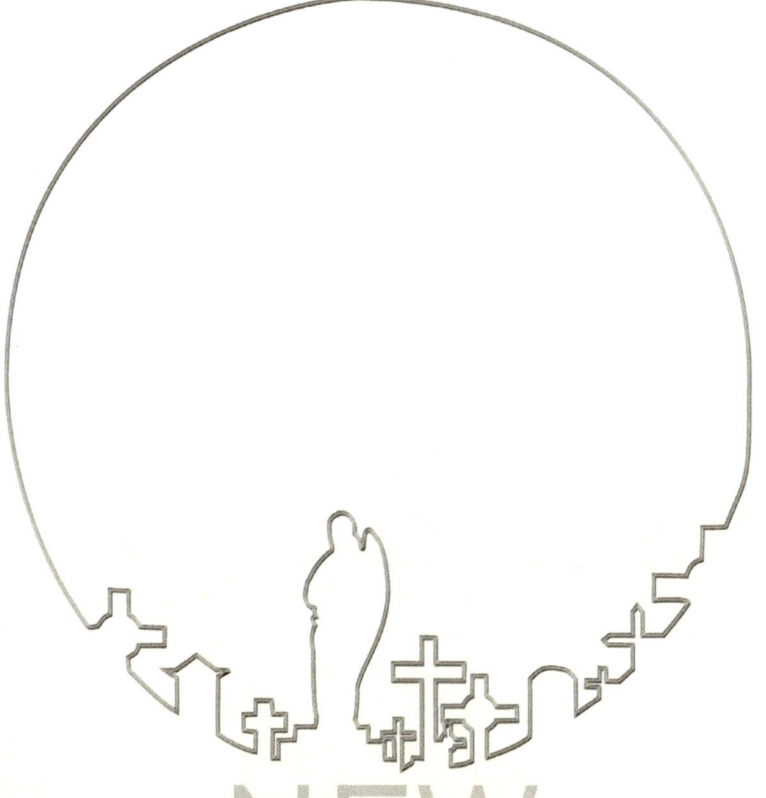

NEW BEGINNINGS

A Ghost Detective Short Story

New Beginnings
by R.W. Wallace

Copyright © 2022 by R.W. Wallace

Cover by R.W. Wallace
Cover Illustration 10926765 © germanjames | 123rf.com
Cover Illustration 2267086 © tdoes1 | Depositphotos
Cover Illustration 192365728 © Natallia Haidutskaya | Dreamstime

This story was first published in *Pulphouse Fiction Magazine*, Issue #17

All characters and events in this book, other than those clearly in the public domain, are fictitious and any resemblance to real persons, living or dead, is purely coincidental.

All rights reserved. No part of this publication may be reproduced, distributed, or transmitted in any form or by any means, including photocopying, recording, or other electronic or mechanical methods, without the prior written permission of the publisher, except in the case of brief quotations embodied in critical reviews and certain other noncommercial uses permitted by copyright law. For permission requests, write to the publisher at the address below.

www.rwwallace.com

ISBN paperback: [978-2-493670-01-4]
ISBN ebook: [978-2-493670-02-1]

First edition

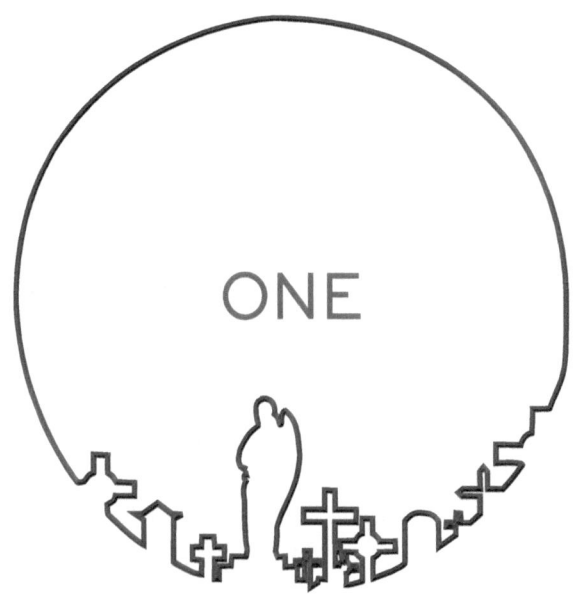

ONE

Everybody dies alone, they say.

No matter how surrounded you are by family and friends in your life, no matter how rich or poor you are, no matter your social status, we're all equal—and alone—in death. Nobody can walk that path with you.

I don't remember my own death, so I find it hard to argue the point, facts in hand.

But I don't like to think that whoever came up with that saying was right.

I can't speak for what happens at the exact moment when someone dies, but I *can* tell you that none of the people who come through our cemetery as ghosts are ever alone.

Clothilde and I are always here to help them adjust to being ghosts, and to help them move on once they've settled whatever unfinished business made them linger.

If either of us ever moves on without the other, whoever remains will, indeed, be lonely. It's something I don't think about all that much anymore—we've both been here for more than thirty years, after all. Chances of either of us figuring out what we need to move on tomorrow are, quite frankly, slim.

It's been the two of us for such a long time, I've come to think of ghosts as belonging in two groups: us and them. Clothilde and I are the constants. The others are only passing through.

When other ghosts come through, we make the effort to get to know them. But we keep a distance, one that we need for our own well-being.

The first years in our cemetery, I befriended most of the other ghosts. Got to know them. What they liked, their sense of humor, their tastes and opinions.

And then they moved on, and left me behind.

Only Clothilde stayed.

So even though the rebellious twenty-year-old with wild, curly hair and worn Converse doesn't seem like the likely friend of a balding thirty-five-year-old washed-out cop, we're the closest thing either of us has to a family.

We're *us*.

And together, we welcome new ghosts—while keeping the required emotional distance.

Today, I think we have a new arrival.

I say *think*, because the signs aren't as clear as usual.

When someone has unfinished business and becomes a ghost, they wake up inside their casket sometime between the ceremony in the church and the moment when the church doors open. Without much surprise, when someone wakes up and discovers they are stuck in a sealed casket, they panic.

Usually, they scream—*we* scream, I was no exception—and pound on the casket, trying to get someone to save them.

This is what alerts us to new arrivals. The large wooden doors to our little stone church squeal open, the mourners pour out and wait on the small area in front of the church, huddling under shared umbrellas if the weather is as wet and depressing as it is today, and then the casket is carried out. Accompanied by screams if the person has become a ghost.

I *think* someone's yelling—but with the murmurs of the large group, the staccato *plops* of rain on umbrellas and gravestones, and the ringing of the church bells, I just can't be sure.

I can't even rule out the possibility of the yells coming from one of the mourners because the rain, the umbrellas, and a large number of hoods make all the people look blurry. This winter has been as depressing as they usually are in this part of France; rain, gray skies, and more rain. Every single day. Not even a single snowflake to brighten things up for a moment or two.

Now that it's finally March, maybe we'll get some sun and fresh spring.

"Is it possible to be too lazy to panic properly when you die?" Clothilde perches on the headstone of her own grave, her feet swinging back and forth, passing through the stone as if it weren't there, her head cocked as she listens for the yells.

"Maybe the rain muffles the sound," I say without conviction. I'm sitting on the small mound marking my own final resting place, very happy that ghosts can't get their pants wet, or feel the cold.

"The rain doesn't muffle ghost sounds," Clothilde replies, but without her usual snark. She's too focused on the casket.

Biting her cheek, she stretches her neck, as if that would help her see anything better from across the cemetery. "I think it's someone old. All the young people are clearly family. If anybody is a friend, they're at least eighty."

That information is probably not *quite* right. Clothilde may have been on this earth for over fifty years—twenty as a normal girl and thirty as a ghost—but her capacity for estimating the age of someone over forty leaves something to be desired.

But as I get up to get a better look myself, I have to concede the point. None of the "friend" mourners are a day under seventy.

"Let's get a little closer," I say, and start walking toward the hole where the casket is to be buried. It's an existing grave in one of the old and fancy parts of the cemetery. The granite slab was removed yesterday to prepare for today's funeral.

I take the narrow paths winding past the gray tombs, glancing at some graves with fresh flowers and regretfully noting the ones that haven't been cleaned in several decades.

Clothilde follows behind while cutting a few corners. She was never one for following the rules of the living when it doesn't suit her. The grave of Monsieur Lopez she cuts through on purpose, like she always does when going through that zone. He spent some time with us as a ghost. Clothilde did not like him.

The burial in itself is pretty straightforward so I don't even bother listening to what the priest says. I go down to crouch down on the casket six feet under to make sure that the sounds I'm hearing are coming from inside.

Polite knocking and the occasional, "Hello? Does anybody hear me?"

Well, that's new.

"Definitely a new arrival, and a polite one at that," I tell Clothilde as I join her in the crowd of mourners.

"There's something weird about this death," Clothilde says. She stands in the middle of the crowd, her hands on her hips, and studies everyone in the vicinity. "And there's something weird about the mourners."

I take the time to look, too. She's right. There's something off about the people around us—but I can't put my finger on what it is.

"What do you mean, there's something weird about the death?" I ask. "From what I understand, the woman was seventy-three, and her husband died and was buried here ten years ago." I find it highly unlikely that the newly arrived Madame Priaux was a murder victim, for example.

Clothilde moves toward a lone woman in her thirties standing somewhat apart from the group in the back. Tears are streaking down her face and this has clearly been going on for a while. Her cheeks are as wet as her raincoat, making it look like the hood has no effect whatsoever.

Clothilde scrutinizes the woman from head to foot several times. "They're too upset."

I fight the urge to roll my eyes—that's usually Clothilde's favorite way of expressing herself. "People are allowed to be upset when they lose someone they love."

Frowning, Clothilde leans in so close to the woman that their noses almost touch. "Not this much. Not for a woman in her seventies who's 'joining her husband.' Not for people who have already lost grandparents, so they know what it's like." She leans back and meets my gaze. "They're shocked this woman is dead."

I make a quick tour around the people present. And conclude that Clothilde is right.

"Maybe it's a familial or cultural thing. They don't deal well with loss?"

Clothilde's reply is a snort. At least she didn't roll her eyes.

The ceremony finished, people mill towards their cars. The young, sad woman remains, and is joined by a man who might be in his early forties. His hair is thinning on top and completely gray around the ears. His beer belly strains his coat around the waist and his black umbrella only covers his front. The back of his jacket is soaked, as are his legs from the knees down.

"Come now, cousin," he says to the woman. "No need to beat yourself up. You did the best you could. It was her time." He holds the umbrella away with one arm and reaches out the other toward the woman's shoulder, clearly to lean in to kiss her cheek.

The woman steps away. "Don't! I might have it."

The man sighs. "You didn't have any symptoms while you were with Mamie for a week, you haven't had any since she died. You're fine. Let me give you a kiss and some human contact. *That* is what we need when we're mourning."

The woman doesn't seem convinced but her cousin doesn't give her much choice. He leans in and kisses her cheek, then retreats back under his umbrella.

"Come," he says to her. "You need to get out of the rain. Can't have you catching your death in this weather." He guffaws at his own joke.

"She died from some kind of contagious disease?" Clothilde says when the two cousins leave the cemetery. "What, like, the flu?"

I can only shrug. We're in France, a country with health care for all and mandatory vaccines. I have to agree with Clothilde. The flu is the only common contagious disease I can think of that would kill an elderly lady like this.

"If that was the flu, then I'll eat a rat," says a shaky voice from behind us.

We rush over to the grave, and find an elderly lady with curled gray hair and thick-rimmed glasses with rhinestones along the top staring up at us, hands on hips.

"Would either of you young people mind telling me how I get out of this pit?"

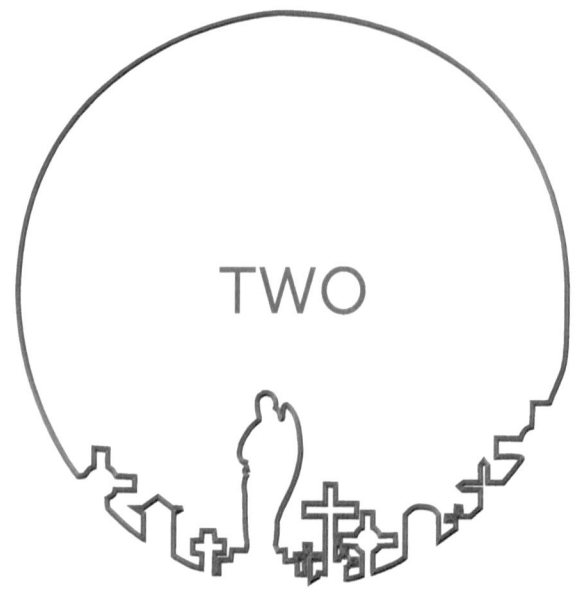

TWO

Her name is Marie-Pierre and she's seventy-three. She used to be a teller in a bank, something she took a break from for fifteen years to raise three children, and eventually went back to when she started feeling claustrophobic in her own home. She has seven grandchildren, one of whom is in great danger of making her a great-grandmother very soon if she doesn't watch out.

"So how did you die?" Clothilde asks. Marie-Pierre didn't feel comfortable sitting on someone else's grave and her own isn't really an option right now, so we've settled on one of the benches under the plane trees. Clothilde is sprawled on the wet ground, ignoring the rain completely, her jeans-clad legs stretched long and arms propped behind her for unneeded support. I'm on the bench with our new colleague, keeping a polite distance.

Marie-Pierre waves a hand in the air. "Some kind of virus. I think. I was quite out of it when they took me to the hospital and although I know they talked about whatever it was around and over me, I didn't really listen." She gets a faraway look and the wrinkles on her forehead deepen. "I was too busy fighting to breathe."

We sit in silence for a while. I have more questions for Maire-Pierre but we're hardly in a rush. She was surprisingly quick to come out of the casket, which might be linked to her age. At some point, people know the end is coming, so it's easier to accept when it happens. Not that seventy-three means a foot in the grave. Rather…well, death is closer than it was yesterday.

"I don't suppose Noël is around?" Marie-Pierre twists around on her bench, scanning the cemetery.

That's the name that was already on the grave Marie-Pierre was buried in. "Was he your husband?" I ask.

"Yes. He died ten years ago. Heart attack from doing too much sport after he retired." She sighs and smiles wistfully. "My mother always told me he was stupid."

"I'm afraid we're the only resident ghosts at this time," I tell her. "Not everybody becomes a ghost, you see. And those who do, don't always linger very long."

Her sharp gaze, too serious for the ridiculous glasses she wears, catches mine. "Yet you've been here for some time."

"Yes. I have." I leave it at that. "Your husband never became a ghost. He must have moved on directly, like the majority of people do. He must not have had any unfinished business."

"Not other than getting up that mountain on his brand new bike," she grumbles. She glances at Clothilde, then back at me. "You are insinuating that I *do* have unfinished business? That's why I'm here?"

Clothilde sits up, wrapping her arms around her knees. "Do you know what it might be?"

Marie-Pierre takes her time thinking about it, cocking her head left and right, grimacing and mumbling to herself.

Finally, she shrugs and folds her hands in her lap. "Nope. Not a clue."

THREE

WE EXPECT MARIE-PIERRE to get visitors once the grave is sealed. Quite often, the people our ghosts have unfinished business with come back, because it's a two-way street.

For two days, not a soul comes to visit—not Marie-Pierre nor anybody else.

On the third day, we get another funeral.

With another new arrival.

This time, there's no doubt. As the church doors open, the screams blow out of the church, loud and male and angry. The pounding on the casket is constant and with several different kinds of resonance—this guy is hitting with both hands and feet. Today, miraculously, there's no rain, so we hear everything perfectly.

"Oh, my," Marie-Pierre says as she slips her glasses down her nose to study the spectacle over their rim. I've tried to explain that she doesn't need glasses anymore, and certainly shouldn't have trouble with focusing on something far away, but the woman just shrugged and adjusted her glasses.

Some habits are hard to kick—and some we don't want to.

We watch from afar as the casket is carried to a newly dug grave in the northeast section and the priest makes a quick sermon.

"Not too many people this time," Clothilde comments. She has abandoned her usual perch to stand on the other side of Marie-Pierre, her arms crossed across her chest and a slight frown on her face.

"Huh," Marie-Pierre says as she yet again lowers her glasses to look at the mourners. "That *is* odd."

"Why?" I ask. We're supposed to be the specialists on funerals and mourners here, not the new arrival.

She points a bony finger at the family standing closest to the grave. A woman in her late fifties and two twenty-something men. They're all blond and stocky.

"That's Lisa and her weird sons. If Didier isn't with her, it means he's the one in the casket." She cocks her head. "Yes, that definitely sounds like Didier." She sends me a look that I'm unable to decipher. "Didier is one of the village's three doctors. He was *my* doctor."

She stops talking but the conversation is clearly continuing in her head. I also see her counting out the number of mourners and mumbling names.

"Everybody loved Didier," she finally says. "He was loud and smart and funny. The entire village should have come to his funeral." She waves at the twenty-five people around the open grave. "This is only family."

I meet Clothilde's gaze over Marie-Pierre's head but my friend just shrugs at me. Village chatter doesn't interest Clothilde.

"Did his family get along well?" I've suddenly realized what seemed odd to *me* about this group—and I think it was the case during Marie-Pierre's funeral, too. "They're not standing very close."

Usually, during a funeral, people huddle close together, seeking human contact.

"They're the closest-knit family I've ever met," Marie-Pierre says, her voice flat. She's realizing something's not right.

She puts a hand on my forearm, either to get my attention or to get that longed-for human contact that is forever denied us ghosts. "What's going on?"

"I don't know," I reply, my voice serious. "I hope Didier will be able to help us figure it out."

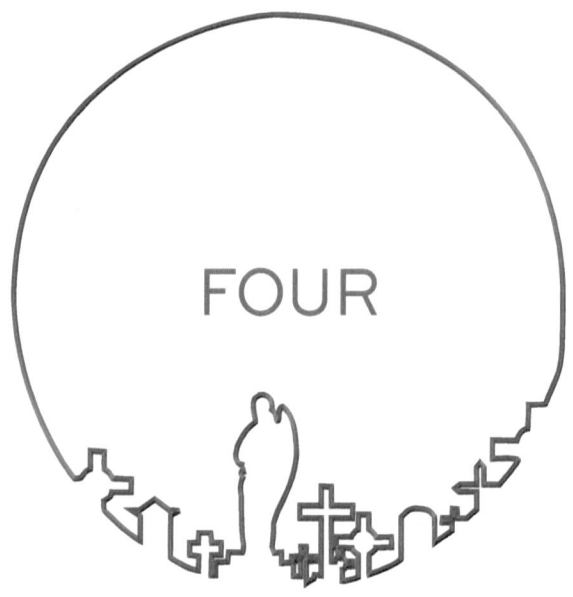

FOUR

Didier emerges from the grave two days later. By then, three new graves have been dug in the southern quadrant of the cemetery and I have a bad feeling in the pit of my stomach that won't go away.

"I can't believe this," are the first words out of his mouth as he crawls out of the grave. "Totally unacceptable." He's a tall man, completely bald, and at least twenty kilos into obese territory. He looks to be in his early sixties.

He catches sight of Marie-Pierre. "Oh, hello Madame Priaux. You're here, too, are you?" Finally free of the dirt, he straightens and stretches his back, then frowns as he realizes this doesn't have its usual effect on his body.

Ghosts don't get back pains—and we can't enjoy a good stretch.

"I'm Robert Villemur," I say, not wanting to wait for the man to ask the questions. "And this is Clothilde. Do you know what's going on? What was your cause of death? That of Marie-Pierre?"

I almost add the three empty graves but decide against it.

Didier gives me a once-over but he doesn't ask any questions. It may appear that if Marie-Pierre is working with me, then I'm okay.

"There's a new virus," he says. "Spreads like wildfire. Attacks the lungs. Especially dangerous to the elderly and those with pre-existing conditions."

He stares daggers at his bulging belly, as if it is the cause of his demise.

"What..." I trail off as I don't even know what to ask him. And even if a killer virus in the world of the living would be a disaster, I'm naturally more turned toward its effect on our ghostly world.

I've talked quite a bit with Marie-Pierre these last couple of days and I cannot figure out what her unfinished business is. If we don't know what the problem is, we can't solve it, and we can't send her off to the other side.

I hold up a hand, palm out. "I want to hear more about this virus, Monsieur, but I have one other pressing question first. Do you happen to know if you have any unfinished business with the living that might be keeping you from moving on?"

"Moving on." Didier turns in a circle to take in our little cemetery. "You mean this isn't the final stop?"

"Next to last," Clothilde says from her perch on a nearby mausoleum. "The one where you can tie up those last loose ends."

Didier nods a greeting to Clothilde. "Mademoiselle. Didn't see you there."

"From what I've understood, Didier," Marie-Pierre says as she pushes her rhinestone glasses up her nose, "ghosts only linger when something is keeping them back. Finding the person who murdered them, speaking to a loved one one last time. Apologizing to estranged family members. Personally, I can't think of anything, but then my mind isn't what it used to be, so maybe I've forgotten?"

"That doesn't seem likely," I hasten to reassure her.

Didier shifts from foot to foot, his forehead creased into a giant frown while he considers the question. "Can't really think of anything." His voice is soft. "Wouldn't mind seeing my family again, but they know I love them. Got along with everyone. And it wasn't a person who killed me, it was this blasted virus."

Could their unfinished business really be with the virus? How is that supposed to work? How can a group of ghosts in a cemetery fight something as intangible as a virus?

I look toward Clothilde but her gaze is turned in direction the parking lot.

Two hearses just arrived.

FIVE

"It's the Moulins," Didier says. There's a fatality to his tone that makes me think he's not surprised to see this particular family.

As the two caskets are pushed toward the church, three other cars arrive, with five people in each car. I assume they're the living members of the Moulin family. They vary in both shapes and sizes, ages and color. One of the men in the last car, a man who must be well past fifty, has a dry cough and leans heavily on a man I assume to be his son as they follow the caskets.

"You're not supposed to come out if you're sick!" Didier yells at the man. "Protect the rest of your disease-ridden family, man!"

Didier faces me, fire in his eyes. "What are the rules here? They can't hear me, I suppose? Can I touch? What can I do?"

"They can neither see, hear, or feel you," I say. "And you can't leave the confines of the cemetery. But sometimes their subconscious *can* get our messages. So it's always worth a shot, but it takes patience."

Didier is studying me a lot closer all of a sudden. "Have we met?" he asks, frowning fiercely. "I didn't catch your name."

"Robert Villemur," I reply.

"The cop," Didier says. "I remember when you went missing."

My eyebrows shoot up and if I'd still had a beating heart, it would have sped up considerably. It's the first time another ghost has recognized me, in all my thirty years in this place.

I'm not buried with the rest of my family. I've never had visitors. I don't even have a proper tombstone, just a slight bump in the grass next to Clothilde's grave.

I have no idea if anybody who cares even knows I'm buried here.

I'm about to say as much when my attention is drawn to the two new caskets. "They're not going into the church?"

The procession is almost all the way to the newly dug graves already, the Moulin family trailing behind. The priest, walking ahead of the caskets, and the funeral agents managing the caskets, are all wearing masks and plastic gloves.

"There's less chance of the virus spreading outdoors," Didier says, before running toward the coughing man.

The rest of us follow at a more leisurely pace.

"The entire family has a tendency to attract all types of diseases," Maire-Pierre says in a low voice. "Diabetes, high blood pressure, pneumonia, cancer. You name the disease, one of the Moulins will have it. Every time I went to Didier's office for an appointment I would meet at least one of them."

Didier is speaking directly into the ear of the man with the cough, trying to convince him to stay away from his other family members. He also yells at the whole group to keep their distance.

When the two caskets are lowered into the ground, Didier comes back to join us. "It's Gérard and Claude," he says to Marie-Pierre. "Two elderly brothers," he adds for my benefit. "The fathers or uncles to most of the people here."

We watch in silence as the priest holds his sermon at the graveside instead of inside the church. I'm fascinated to participate in this part of the funeral for the first time since my own demise. Usually, we only get the last words once the casket is in the ground.

I learn something new, too: ghosts wake up when the mass is over. Everybody echoes the priest's "Amen," and the yells start.

"Gérard! Where are you? What is going on?"

"Claude? Where am I? Why is it so dark?"

Clothilde glances up at me and curls her upper lip.

Two more ghosts.

SIX

For two weeks, we continue down the same slippery slope.

Six more funerals, six more ghosts—and fewer and fewer mourners attending the funerals.

We've received the coughing man from the Moulin family, and the overconfident cousin from Marie-Pierre's funeral, the one who insisted on kissing the cheek of the woman who'd spent time taking care of the sick Marie-Pierre.

Marie-Pierre was devastated to discover he'd died—and then proceeded to give the man the talking-to of a lifetime for taking such a big threat so lightly.

For the last funeral, the final journey of one Mathilde Joubert, the thirty-six-year-old cashier at the local Lidl, only her mother shows up to say her goodbyes.

When Mathilde crawls out of the grave four days later, there are twelve ghosts waiting for her.

I've sat down with all our new arrivals over the past weeks, digging into their histories and reasons for becoming ghosts. With the possible exception of a man who hasn't seen his children in over a decade, I find no unfinished business we need to settle, no reason for all of them to linger.

Except the virus.

But what can I possibly do about this thing from the confines of our cemetery? What could I do even *outside* of the cemetery? I don't know how to defeat a virus. I don't know how to bring it to justice.

When we go a week without any new funerals, I tentatively hope we've seen the worst of it. Ten deaths within a month is a very high number for such a small village.

Ten ghosts for ten deaths has never happened—at least not in my thirty years.

Clothilde and I have started taking daily walks around the cemetery, just the two of us, to get away from the others for a while.

We've been used to it being just the two of us for so long, it's hard to adapt to having enough ghosts to make up an entire soccer team. So we take these walks, and pretend we're back to normal for a short hour every day.

"You think the gardener will be back soon?" Clothilde asks as we step through the growing weeds along the west wall.

I run a hand through the pale purple wisteria adorning the cemetery wall, wishing I could still smell their sweet scent. "The lockdown is apparently scheduled to end in two weeks," I say. "I'm guessing our gardener will be back then."

Right now, with nobody doing any kind of upkeep while the spring sun is shining beautifully, our cemetery is looking more and more abandoned by the day.

Or like an overgrown English garden.

I'm starting to think that nature gaining turf might not be such a bad thing.

Apparently, outside, the entire world has shut down in order to stop the virus from spreading. Schools are closed, restaurants are closed, concerts are canceled, people are working from home…. And everyone is sheltering in place, waiting for the plague to pass.

Yet in our cemetery, everything is the same.

Except for the growing weeds—and the ten extra ghosts.

And the lack of visitors.

"We haven't had a single visitor since this all started with Marie-Pierre's funeral," I say. "Do you think that could be what sets them free? They need to say proper goodbyes to the people they left behind?"

Clothilde shrugs. "Except for that one guy, they don't seem to feel too strong a need to say goodbye. And for *all* of them to feel that way?" She trails off and jumps up to walk on the wall. Well, she's walking on air right *next* to the wall—we can't cross the middle of the stone construction.

"I don't like having so many people here," she says as she carefully puts one foot ahead of the other, arms out for balance—as if there's any risk of her falling down.

"I know," I say.

Ironic, really, that we should spend so much time worrying about being all alone and then complain when we finally have company.

"The visitors should come back once the lockdown is over," I say. "Maybe we'll get some answers then."

And in the meantime, we'll try to pretend to be extroverts and enjoy the new company.

SEVEN

Mid-May, under a beautifully clear and blue sky, with the sun shining down on the living and dead alike, the lockdown is lifted.

Everybody gets visitors on the very first day. Clothilde and I were feeling crowded with ten extra ghosts—now add in hundreds of live visitors.

Clothilde turns into a gloomy teenager and follows some of the louder visitors around, telling them to be quiet and testing their sensibility to ghosts to determine if there is any point in attempting a prank.

I leave her to it.

I decide to join Marie-Pierre at her grave when her daughter comes with a bouquet of orange roses.

"They're from the garden," the middle-aged woman says. "You always seemed to love to come visit when that rose bush was in bloom." She looks to be in her fifties and is wearing a pair of washed-out jeans and a simple black T-shirt. Her hair is short and has dark blue highlights.

Marie-Pierre caresses her daughter's cheek with the backs of her fingers. "I loved to come visit any time." Her hand goes to the blue streaks. "When did you do this?"

The daughter must be sensitive to ghosts because her hand goes to her hair. "I got so bored during the lockdown," she says with a wistful smile. "Figured a little color in my life wouldn't hurt."

Marie-Pierre seems happy.

But she's not fading. Seeing her daughter again and having the chance to say goodbye is clearly not going to be enough for her to move on.

Someone seems to be causing a scene near the parking lot.

At first, I figure it's the live people—they outnumber us at least one to five, after all—but then I realize only the ghosts are reacting. Marie-Pierre is lowering her glasses to look toward the noise, and I see Didier straightening from where he was crouching next to a young girl at his own grave.

It's the beer-bellied cousin.

"What is that idiot Vincent up to now," Marie-Pierre says under her breath as she pushes her glasses back up her nose.

"Looks like he's not happy with his cousin," I say. "The

woman who cared for you before you died?" I think that's her coming through the main gate right now and even though I can't make out the words, the anger and fury in Vincent's voice carries and clashes with such a beautiful sunny day as he hovers over her and yells straight into her face.

I rush to the poor woman's rescue but Clothilde gets there before me.

We might not have physical forms but we remember how things used to work. So when Vincent receives Clothilde's angry eyes right in front of his own face, he takes a step back.

"*What* is your problem?" Clothilde hisses.

The live woman draws a shaky breath and runs a hand down her face but she keeps moving, toward Marie-Pierre's grave if I'm not mistaken.

"What is my problem?" Vincent is not backing down from Clothilde and even goes to far as to try to push her away.

His hands go right through her.

He recovers quickly, though. "My problem is that I'm dead because of that woman. She had the virus and gave it to me and now I'm dead!"

"That's hardly fair, Vincent," Marie-Pierre says. She has joined us by the main gate. There's an entire area that the living are currently avoiding, though none of them will realize it's because there's a fight between ghosts going on.

Marie-Pierre shows she has learned to master the rules of being a ghost as she stands on thin air to get right into her grandson's face. "If she had the virus, it was because she caught it from me. Does this mean you are blaming me for your death?"

"Well…no, of course not," Vincent stammers. "It's not like you gave it to her on purp—"

"Did she go out of her way to give it to you? Cough into your face? Touch your hands?"

I see the moment Vincent thinks he's found a way out. "At your funeral, she—"

"She told you not to get near her," I say. "And yet you insisted on kissing her cheek anyway."

He sputters some more, until he realizes there's now a total of ten ghosts surrounding him, and not a one who seems likely to take his side.

Finally, he mutters, "So you're saying it's *my* fault."

Marie-Pierre tuts at him and pats his cheek. "It's nobody's fault, Vincent. *C'est la vie.*"

I can tell from her expression that Clothilde wants to point out that it's actually death, but luckily, she refrains.

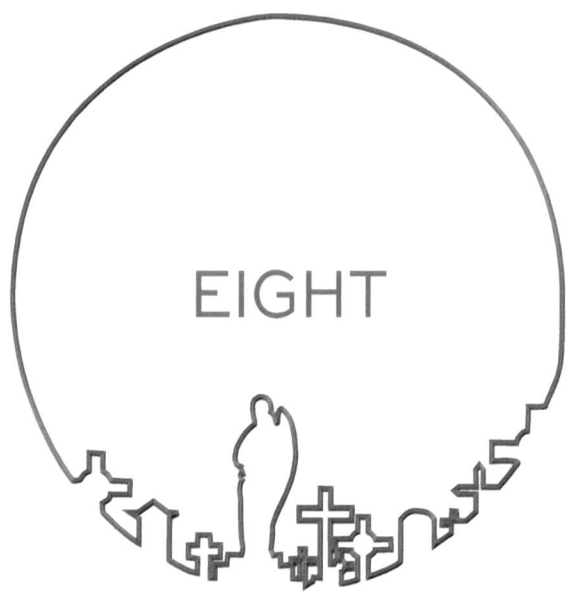

EIGHT

As the cemetery is closed for the night, all the ghosts gather around Marie-Pierre's grave. Being the only one buried in an already existing grave, she's the only of the new arrivals with an actual tombstone, albeit still without her name on it. Some are sitting on the large slab of granite covering the tomb, others are standing on the path. Clothilde is perched on a neighboring headstone.

I'm off to one side, arms crossed and feet wide. I know the stance is a little aggressive but not figuring out what everybody needs is getting on my nonexistent nerves.

"Did everyone get visitors today?" I ask the group, and they nod or reply in the affirmative with expressions ranging from grinning to worried frowns.

"Yet nobody moved on." I tried making time for everyone throughout the day, to listen in on their "conversations" with their loved ones, but still, nothing jumped out as an obvious reason for lingering.

With one notable exception. "Vincent," I say, "I think if you can forgive your cousin for giving you the virus, or accept your part of the responsibility, that might be enough."

After a quick glance at the glaring Marie-Pierre, he mumbles, "There's nothing to forgive. It was nobody's fault."

Right. Now what?

As the last sunlight disappears below the horizon, we sit in silence. I'm all out of ideas and cannot even imagine what living in this cemetery will be like if we're going to be twelve instead of two.

"It's a beautiful night," Marie-Pierre comments. "So odd, that the world keeps turning without us."

"All my patients will have to find a new doctor," Didier says.

"Our kids are going to fight over those houses we own together for decades," Gérard says, and his brother Claude nods.

"My cousin is going to feel guilty about my death forever." Vincent hangs his head.

"So the world keeps turning," Marie-Pierre says. "But not quite the same way."

"A worse way," Vincent says.

"Nonsense." Marie-Pierre's voice has lost its wistfulness. She's dead serious. "It's different, not worse. This virus has changed the world. But change isn't always worse, or better. It's different, and new."

"And it will be different and new without us." Didier's words could be taken as depressing or fatalistic, but his tone is anything but. It sounds like he's made a happy discovery.

Like a responsibility has been lifted.

He throws out his arms to indicate the cemetery around us. "We have a new world to discover. Together."

The mood shift for the entire group comes slowly, but clearly. They're letting go of the anger at having died from some invisible virus they had no control over. They tell each other how happy they are to see that their living relatives seem to be safe and doing well.

And they plan ahead. As a group.

I walk over to stand beside Clothilde. "I think they're planning to stay," I say, low enough that none of the others will overhear.

"Over my dead body." Then Clothilde throws her head back and cackles a loud laugh.

When she calms down, she pats my shoulder. "Don't worry, it won't come to that." She lifts her chin toward the group of ghosts. "They're already leaving."

She's right.

In a large group on the path now, they're slowly becoming transparent. Didier notices first. "What does this mean?"

"You're moving on," I say.

"You're not," Marie-Pierre says.

I shrug. "That's all right. You take care of each other."

Excitement and fear cross their faces as they fade. They grab each other's hands mere seconds before they all disappear.

Silence.

Night has fallen but we can somehow still see each other.

"Wanna go hang out on my grave?" Clothilde says as she jumps down from her perch.

"Always." I follow slowly, reclaiming my cemetery and taking my time to enjoy the return to normal.

And sending up an extra thanks for having my friend here with me.

See? Nobody is alone in death.

Also by R.W. Wallace

Mystery

Ghost Detective Novels
Beyond the Grave
Unveiling the Past
Beneath the Surface
Piercing the Veil

Ghost Detective Shorts
Just Desserts
Lost Friends
Family Bonds
Common Ground
Till Death
Family History
Heritage
New Beginnings
Far From Home
Severed Ties
Eternal Bond
Harsh Expectations
Dull Expectations

Ghost Detective Collections
Unfinished Business, Vol 1

The Tolosa Mystery Series
The Red Brick Haze
The Red Brick Cellars
The Red Brick Basilica

Short Story Collections
Deep Dark Secrets
A Thief in the Night

Romance

French Office Romance Series
Flirting in Plain Sight
Hiding in Plain Sight

Standalone Novels
Love at First Flight

Holiday Stories

Collections
Heartwarming Holiday Tales

Short Stories
The Case of the Disappearing Gingerbread City
Crooks and Nannies

Young Adult Short Story Collections
Tales From the Trenches

Find all R.W. Wallace's books:

rwwallace.com/allbooks

ABOUT THE AUTHOR

R.W. WALLACE WRITES in most genres, though she tends to end up in mystery more often than not. Dead bodies keep popping up all over the place whenever she sits down in front of her keyboard.

The stories mostly take place in Norway or France; the country she was born in and the one that has been her home for two decades. Don't ask her why she writes in English—she won't have a sensible answer for you.

Her Ghost Detective short story series appears in *Pulphouse Magazine*, starting in issue #9.

You can find all her books, long and short, all genres, on rwwallace.com.

www.ingramcontent.com/pod-product-compliance
Lightning Source LLC
LaVergne TN
LVHW040203080526
838202LV00042B/3303